WE'RE GOING ON A
LION HUNT

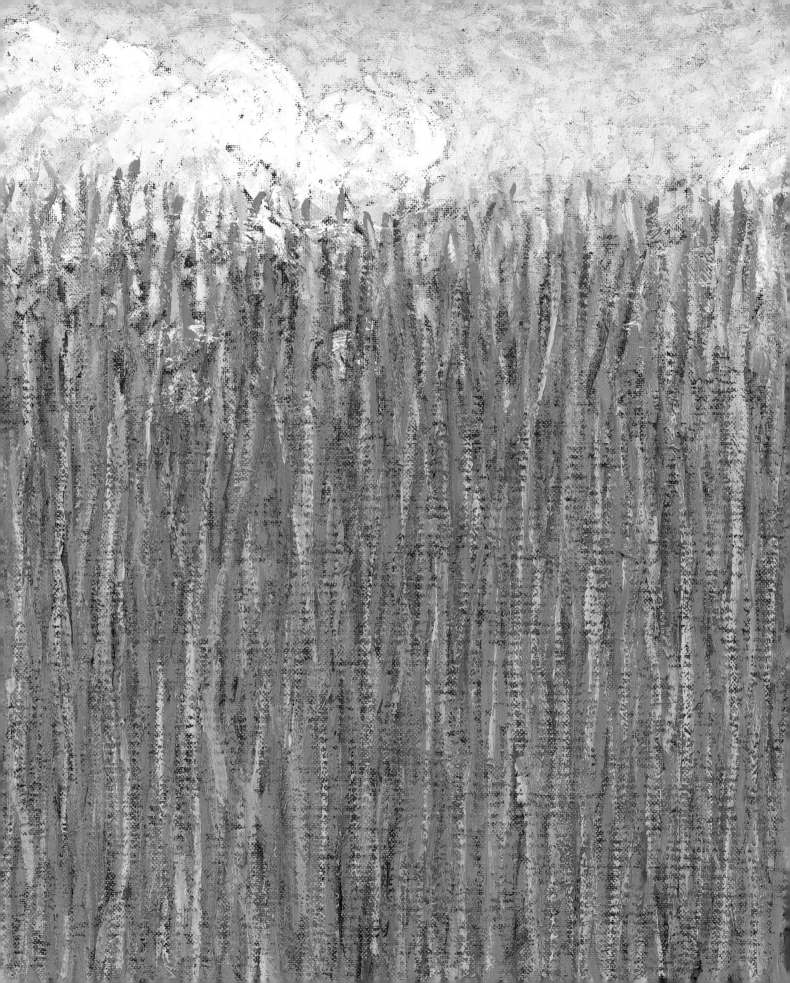

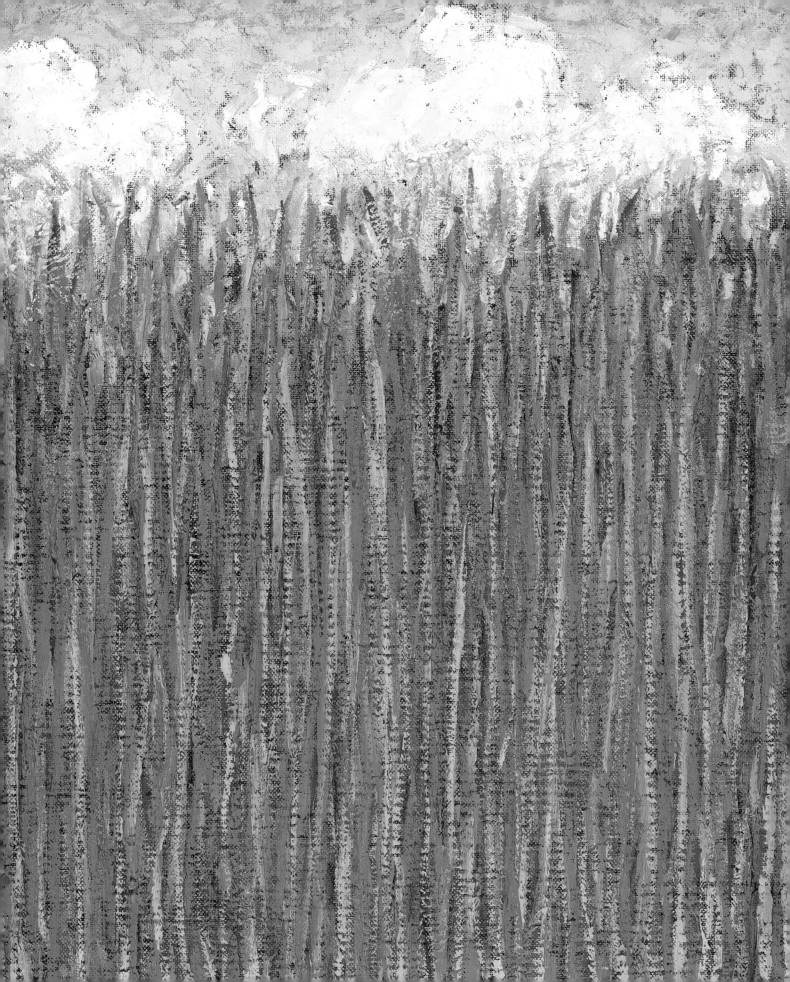

For Chantelle and Sophie

First published 1999 by Macmillan Children's Books
This edition published 2000 by Macmillan Children's Books
a division of Macmillan Publishers Limited
20 New Wharf Road, London N1 9RR
Basingstoke and Oxford
Associated companies throughout the world

ISBN: 978-0-333-74149-8

Text copyright © Macmillan Publishers Limited 1999
Illustrations copyright © David Axtell 1999

The right of David Axtell to be identified as the illustrator of this work has
been asserted by him in accordance with the Copyright, Designs and Patents Act 1988.

21 23 25 24 22 20

A CIP catalogue record for this book is available from the British Library.

Printed in China

WE'RE GOING ON A
LION HUNT

Illustrated by David Axtell

MACMILLAN CHILDREN'S BOOKS

W e're going on a lion hunt.
We're going to catch a big one.
We're not scared.
Been there before.

We're going on a lion hunt.

We're going to catch a big one.

We're not scared.

Been there before.

Oh no . . .

Long grass!

Can't go *over* it.

Can't go *under* it.

Can't go *around* it.

Have to go *through* it.

Swish, swash, swish, swash.

We're going on a lion hunt.

We're going to catch a big one.

We're not scared.

Been there before.

Oh no . . .

A lake!

Can't go *over* it.

Can't go *under* it.

Can't go *around* it.

Have to go *through* it.

Splish, splash, splish, splash.

We're going on a lion hunt.

We're going to catch a big one.

We're not scared.

Been there before.

Oh no . . .

A swamp!

Can't go *over* it.

Can't go *under* it.

Can't go *around* it.

Have to go *through* it.

Squish, squelch, squish, squelch.

We're going on a lion hunt.

We're going to catch a big one.

We're not scared.

Been there before.

Oh no . . . a big dark cave!

Can't go *over* it.

Can't go *under* it.

Can't go *around* it.

Have to go *through* it.

In we go,

Tiptoe, tiptoe!

But what's that?

One shiny wet nose!

One big shaggy mane!

Four big furry paws!

It's a lion!

Back through the cave!
Tiptoe, tiptoe.

Back through the swamp!

Squish, squelch, squish, squelch.

Back through the lake!

Splish, splash, splish, splash.

Back through the long grass!

Swish, swash, swish, swash.

All the way home!

Slam the door!

Crash!

We're all tired now.
Tired and sleepy.

Better catch a lion tomorrow instead!

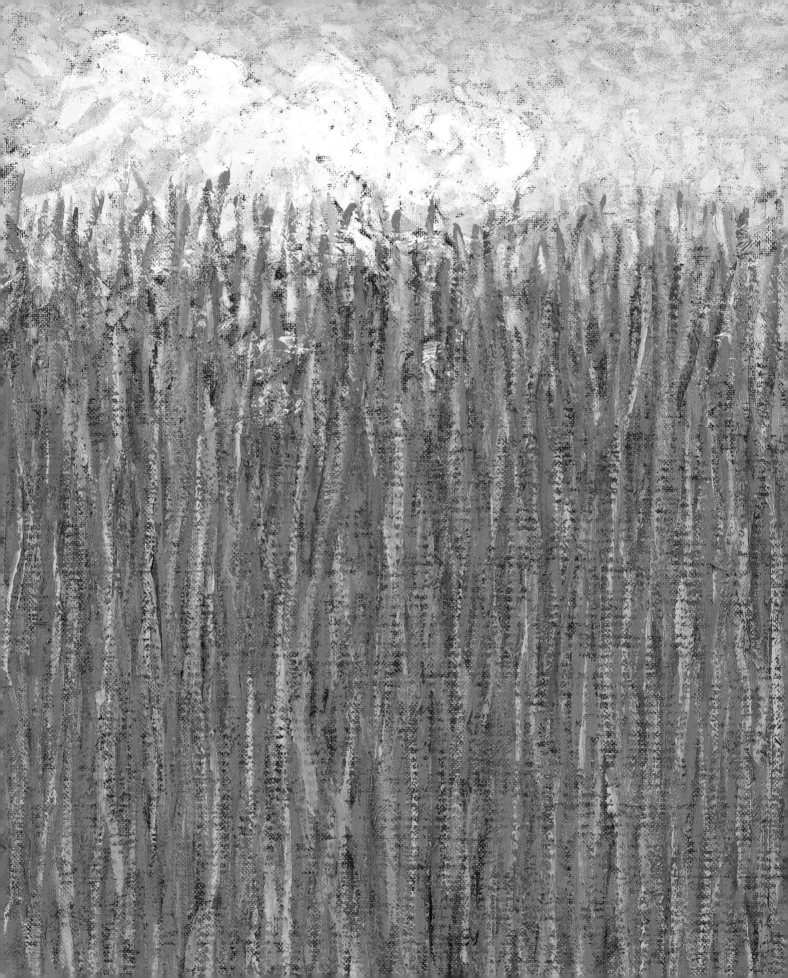

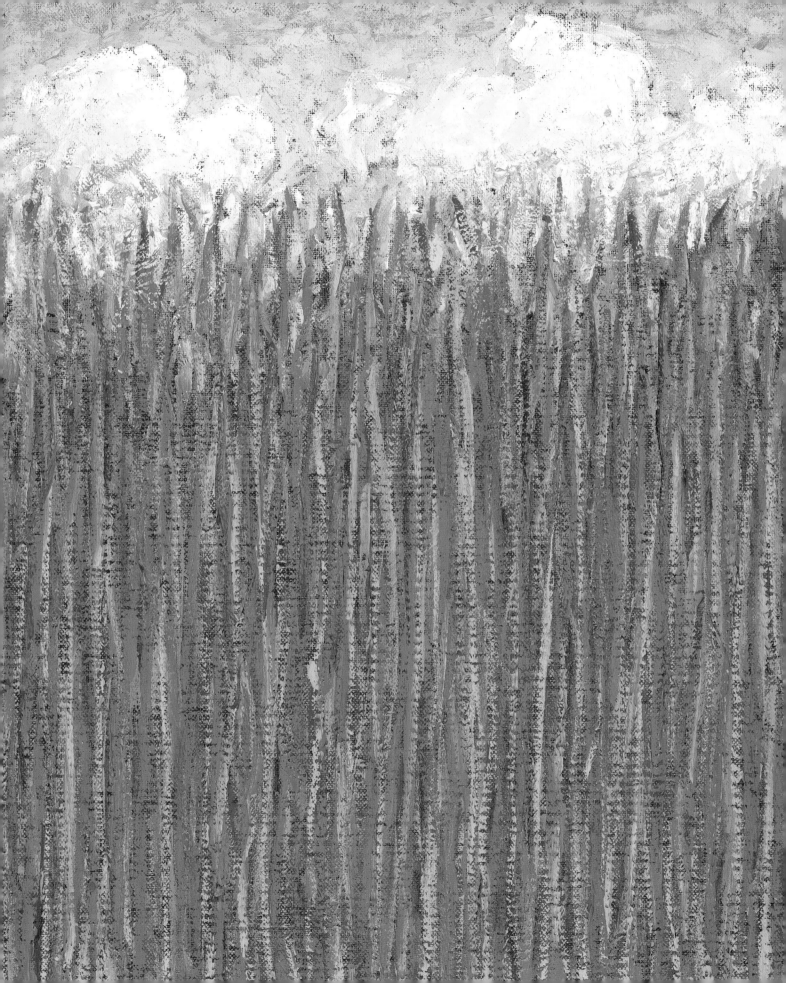